Truck Pals on the Job

Hal & Al

written and illustrated by Ken Bowser

RED
CHAIR
•PRESS•

Funny Bone Readers and Funny Bone Books are published by Red Chair Press
Red Chair Press LLC   PO Box 333   South Egremont, MA 01258-0333
www.redchairpress.com

For my Grandson, Liam Hayden Bowser
who never met a truck he didn't like.

Publisher's Cataloging-In-Publication Data
Bowser, Ken.

  Hal & Al / written and illustrated by Ken Bowser.

   pages : illustrations ; cm. -- (Funny bone readers. Truck pals on the job)

   Summary: Hal has worked in the warehouse a very long time. Will his loyalty
be put to the test when a new machine shows up?

   Interest age level: 004-008.

   ISBN: 978-1-63440-068-8 (library hardcover)

   ISBN: 978-1-63440-069-5 (paperback)

   Issued also as an ebook. (ISBN: 978-1-63440-070-1)

   1. Forklift trucks--Juvenile fiction. 2. Loyalty--Juvenile fiction. 3. Teams in the
workplace--Juvenile fiction. 4. Friendship--Juvenile fiction. 5. Forklift trucks--Fiction.
6. Loyalty--Fiction. 7. Teams in the workplace--Fiction. 8. Friendship--Fiction. I. Title.
II. Title: Hal and Al

PZ7.B697 Ha 2016

[E]   2015938001

Printed in the United States of America
Distributed in the U.S. by Lerner Publisher Services. www.lernerbooks.com

1015 1P WRZSP16

It was busy day at the main warehouse.
Heavy boxes needed to be moved. Big
crates needed to be lifted into place.
A new shipment had arrived.

"I need to stay on my wheels today!" thought Hal. "Being the one and only forklift in the main warehouse is a big responsibility!" he thought to himself.

Foreman Frank handed Hal his
morning work order.
"I'll get right to it!" he said.

Hal sputtered and puffed and squeaked
as he worked. He loved working the
main floor. He knew his way around
the warehouse better than anyone.

"I know where everything goes and
just how to stack it!" Hal boasted.
"I can hoist heavy boxes and crates
and put them right where they go."

Hal lifted the blue boxes from the lower shelf like his work order said. Next Hal moved them all the way up to the top shelf. "There, that's good!" he said.

Then Hal lifted the huge red boxes
from the middle shelf and placed them
on the warehouse floor. "That was
simple," he puffed.

After his morning break it was time to move to the loading dock to organize the new shipment. Hal whistled a tune on the way.

The loading dock was an exciting place.
Big trucks came and stacked boxes.
Tiny boxes were moved by Dolly and
the other hand trucks.

Hal moved all of the big cardboard boxes over to the "New Arrivals" section. "There," he said. "That takes care of that!" he said with a sputter.

Then he moved all of the pallets of other boxes over to the "Receiving" section. "That was a breeze," he clanked.

When he was done with the pallets Hal raced to where all of the newly arrived wooden crates were located.

"Okay!" he thought. "Now to move these wooden crates over to the 'New Crate' section." He worked for hours and only had to take one long break.

Hal came to the last crate. "What is this?" he thought. *Automatic Robotic Forklift* the label read. Hal was puzzled. "A new fork lift?" he worried. "Huh?"

"Better watch out, Hal!" Buff the buffer said. "You can be replaced by a robot! It happened to my uncle Biff in Detroit." "Yeah," Dolly said. "Better watch it!"

"They got a new forklift?" Hal wondered out loud. "Why would they replace me? I do a great job. I work really hard," he sighed. Hal was sad.

Suddenly the crate opened and out rolled the AL 5000. "I...AM...AL...," the thing said in a robot voice. "I... NEVER...NEED...A...BREAK...," it whirred.

"I...CAN...LIFT...1,000...POUNDS...,"
it buzzed. The robot rolled with hardly
a sound. No puffing. No sputtering.
"1,000 pounds? No breaks?"
I'm doomed!" thought Hal.

Suddenly the warehouse door swung open. "Ah! The AL 5000 is finally here!" Foreman Frank smiled as he entered. "Just what we've needed!" "Oh, no!" Hal moaned.

"Hal, meet your new helper!"
Frank said. "Al's here to assist you
and you'll be his boss!"
"You mean, you're... you're not
replacing me?" Hal said with a grin.

"Replacing YOU?" Frank laughed loudly. "We could NEVER replace you, Hal! You know this place better than anyone!" Frank said and they all laughed.

Big Questions: Why do you think Hal was worried about the robot AL? Do you think Hal worked hard at his job? Was Foreman Frank happy with Hal's work? How do you know?

Big Words:

warehouse: a large building where items are kept before being used or sold

pallet: a wooden platform items are kept on to be moved from one place to another